Blue Corn Soup

Caroline Stutson Illustrated by Teri Weidner

PUBLISHED BY SLEEPING BEAR PRESS

Whiskers wiggle. Eyes grow bright.
Mouse peeks out. The canyon's white.
Snow—she blinks. She'll grind dried corn.
Blue corn soup will keep her warm.

Abuelita fills her pot.
She'll make *sopa*—not a lot;
just enough for one small mouse,
cozy in her sagebrush house.

Piñon smoke drifts through the wood.
Someone's cooking something good.

Chipmunk chatters, sniffs about.
Is it *sopa*? He'll find out.

Abuelita stirs her pot.
The *sopa* bubbles, thick and hot.
She will taste a tiny bit.
Something's missing!
What—is—it?

Mouse adds pepper, chop, chop, chop,
into the *sopa* with a plop.
Just enough for one small mouse
staying warm inside her house.

Piñon smoke drifts through the wood.
Someone's cooking something good.

Rabbit bounces, sniffs about.
Is it *sopa*? He'll find out.

Abuelita stirs her pot.
The *sopa* bubbles, thick and hot.
She will taste a tiny bit.
Something's missing!
What—is—it?

Mouse adds pine nuts, chop, chop, chop,
into the *sopa* with a plop.
Just enough for one small mouse
making soup inside her house.

Piñon smoke drifts through the wood.
Someone's cooking something good.

Old Bear grumbles, sniffs about.
Is it *sopa*? He'll find out.

Abuelita stirs her pot.
The *sopa* bubbles, thick and hot.
She will taste a tiny bit.
Something's missing!
What—is—it?

Mouse adds onion, chop, chop, chop,
into the *sopa* with a plop.
Just enough for one small mouse
all alone inside her house.

Piñon smoke drifts through the wood.
Someone's cooking something good.

Is it *sopa*? Neighbors stare.
Three move closer, sniff the air.

"What is this?" Mouse peeks outside.
Whiskers wiggle. Eyes grow wide.
Chipmunk, Rabbit, and Old Bear
smell her *sopa*, want to share.

Abuelita lifts her pot.
Three can tell there's not a lot.
Hungry neighbors turn away.
"No blue *sopa*, not today."

"Wait!" Mouse follows. "We can share.
Bring some food to Old Bear's lair."

When Mouse tips her little pot,
mixed together, there's a lot!

Blue corn *sopa*? More like stew.
Four must name it something new …

"Yes!" Mouse dances.
"Friendship stew!"
Do they like it? Yes, they do.

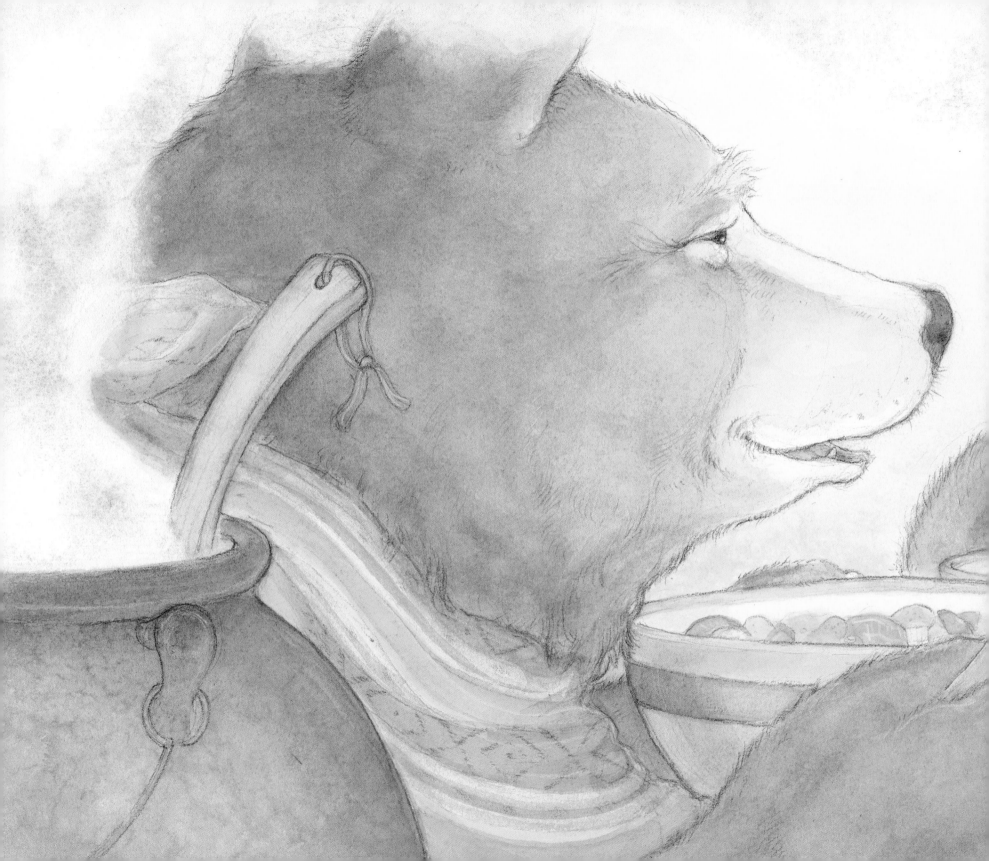

Neighbors gather on the floor,
sip their stew, and ask for more.
Nothing's missing; all can see:
Food tastes best with company.

Snow has dwindled. Small stars light.
Four *amigos* wave good night,
full at last for now at least,
thankful for their harvest feast.

Blue Corn Soup Recipe

2 tablespoons olive oil
2 small onions, chopped
2 cloves garlic, chopped
1 green pepper, chopped
1 teaspoon chili powder
1 teaspoon ground cumin
Salt and pepper to taste
2 tablespoons blue cornmeal
5 cups vegetable broth
1 can (28 ounces) diced tomatoes, with juice
2 cans (15 ounces) black beans, rinsed and drained
2 cups frozen corn
2 cups chopped butternut squash
2 cups chopped potatoes
Toppings: grated cheese, toasted pine nuts

1. Heat oil in a large soup pot. Add onions, garlic, and
   green pepper. Season with chili powder, cumin, salt,
   and pepper. Cook, stirring, until vegetables are soft.
2. Add blue cornmeal, broth, tomatoes, black beans,
   corn, squash, and potatoes. Bring to a simmer, cover
   pot, and cook until squash and potatoes are tender—
   about 40 minutes.
3. Top with cheese and toasted pine nuts.
4. Share with friends.